JASPER & SCRUFF

THE TREASURE HUNT

*For my
very supportive
parents and
husband, Gavin*

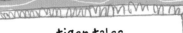

tiger tales

5 River Road, Suite 128, Wilton, CT 06897

Published in the United States 2020

Originally published in Great Britain 2019

by the Little Tiger Group

Text and illustrations copyright © 2019 Nicola Colton

ISBN-13: 978-1-68010-203-1

ISBN-10: 1-68010-203-6

Printed in China

STP/1800/0289/1019

10 9 8 7 6 5 4 3 2 1

For more insight and activities, visit us at
www.tigertalesbooks.com

by Nicola Colton

JASPER
& SCRUFF

THE TREASURE HUNT

tiger tales

J asper was the type of
cat who liked the finer
things in life: fancy meals,
bow ties, and expensive art.

His best friend, Scruff, liked the simpler things: chasing his ball, sniffing out adventures, and eating anything salted-caramel flavor.

Jasper was also the type of cat who had
always dreamed of running a bookstore.

And now he did ...
with the help of Scruff.

One morning, Jasper was counting the money in the register as they waited for the first customers of the day.

"Scruff, I think we've sold even more books than last week," he purred contentedly. "Scruff?"

"Wheeeeee!" cried Scruff as he slid past on a rolling ladder, knocking some books to the floor.

Jasper sighed as he went to pick them up. He had asked Scruff to dust the shelves, but he didn't mean like that!

Ding-a-ling!

A bell rang as the door swung open.

"Be with you in just a minute,"
Jasper called.

A hooded figure tiptoed across
the floor and placed a book-shaped
package lightly on the counter.

Ding-a-ling!

The bell rang again as the figure left. Jasper turned around.

"Scruff," he said, looking down at the package. "Did you see who left this?"

"Wheeeeee!" Scruff zoomed past again.

Jasper carefully tore open the paper
to reveal a leather-bound book.

"Black Whiskers," he said, tracing his
paw over the fancy lettering on the cover.

Scruff leaped down from the ladder
and skidded across the counter.

"The pirate?" he panted.

"Ugh! You're getting drool on my bow tie," groaned Jasper, dabbing at it with his hanky.

"Well? What does it say?" asked Scruff.

Jasper opened the book and began to read.

Black Whiskers was Captain of the *Silver Sardine*. A skilled treasure hunter, she discovered riches all over the world. It was said that she used up most of her nine lives battling storms and fighting sea monsters. She set out on her last voyage to Dogtooth Island in search of the legendary Golden Bone. But she never returned....

"Wow!" said Scruff, his tail wagging.
"I heard that her first mate
stole the Golden Bone."

As Jasper turned the page, a yellowing
sheet of paper floated to the ground.

"Look!" yapped Scruff.
"A treasure map."

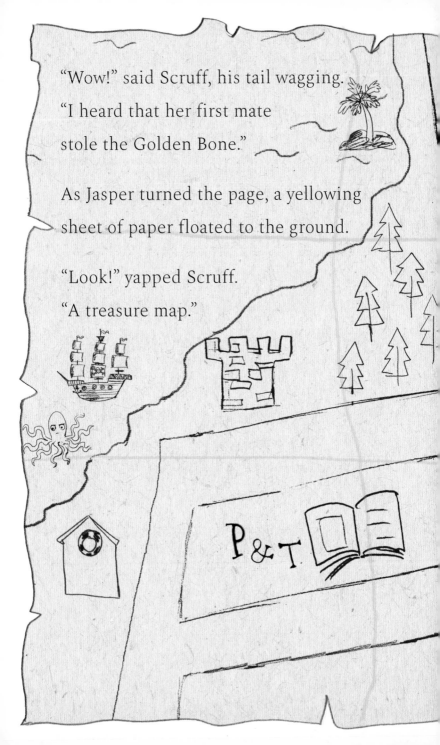

On the hour
you will hear my song.
So hurry up now and
move along.

"The Golden Bone!" whispered Jasper. His eyes became as large as saucers of cream as he imagined adding it to his art collection.

But as Jasper picked up the map, Scruff grabbed the other end between his teeth.

"Grrrr," growled the puppy playfully. Tug-of-war was one of his favorite games!

"Scruff, let go. You're going to tear it," said Jasper.

Riiiiiiip!

Jasper stumbled backward into a display of books. "Ow!" he yelped.

"Ack!" spluttered Scruff, coughing up a piece of the map.

Jasper smoothed out the crumpled map on the counter. Then he picked up the soggy scrap with his hanky and put it in its place.

"It looks like a map of our town," said Jasper, twiddling his whiskers thoughtfully. "But how could the Golden Bone have ended up here?"

Jasper grabbed his magnifying glass to take a closer look. "Ah, there's something written beside Mrs. Caw's clock shop," he said. "It could be a clue. *On the hour you will hear my song. So hurry up now and move along.*"

"It's almost ten o'clock now,"
said Scruff. "Let's go!"

"What about the store?"
asked Jasper.

"Oh, come on. It'll be fun!" said Scruff.
"I'll make a sign to let everyone know
we'll be back soon."

"Hmmm, I guess...," said Jasper.

"Yay! An adventure! I love adventures," said
Scruff as he ducked behind the counter.

A few minutes later, he reappeared
waving a sign and wearing a large hat.

"Um, Scruff … what's that?"

"It's my pirate hat. Do you like it?"
Scruff said. "I even managed to tuck
my treasure-hunting kit inside."

"It's certainly, um ... interesting,"
said Jasper.

As Scruff hung his sign on the door,
Jasper looked for the key to lock up the
store. But it wasn't in its usual spot.

THE PAW & TAIL

"Scruff, did you move the key?"
he asked.

Scruff shook his head.

"Oh, well," said Jasper, plucking a
spare key from under a plant pot.

There was no time to lose, so the pair took a shortcut through the park. As they got closer to Mrs. Caw's shop, they could hear music.

"Morning, Mrs. Caw," said Scruff,
bounding inside.

"Shoobie doobie doo, you're my
weekend bird...," crowed Mrs. Caw as
she polished a display case.

Jasper snapped along to the music.
Alvis Pawsley was his favorite singer.

"Do you have any clocks that sing
on the hour?" asked Scruff.

"Oh, hello there," said Mrs. Caw,
turning down the record player.
"A clock with some flowers, you say?"

"Um, no, a clock that sings on the
hour," repeated Jasper.

"Sings? Hmm…," said Mrs. Caw, resting her beak on her wing. "We've got Tickers and Tockers, Chimers and Buzzers, Dingers and Dongers, but no singing clocks. We do have one that goes—"

Cuckoo!

Jasper almost jumped out of his fur.

"Yes, that's the one," said Mrs. Caw,
pointing up at a cuckoo clock.

"Look, something just fell out of the
cuckoo's beak," said Scruff.

"You don't mind if we take that,
do you?" asked Jasper.

Outside, Jasper unfolded
the piece of paper.

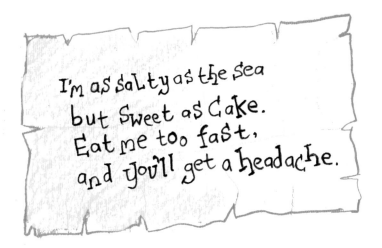

I'm as salty as the sea
but sweet as cake.
Eat me too fast,
and you'll get a headache.

"Mmmm, I know this one!" Scruff
licked his lips. "It has to be Salty Sid's
salted caramel ice cream."

"Really?" said Jasper. "Are you sure?"
This clue seemed a little easy.

"If I'm wrong, we can still
have ice cream!" said Scruff.

"All right," said Jasper.
"But Salty Sid's is miles away."

"Why don't we ask Mrs. Caw if we can borrow her tandem bike?" suggested Scruff.

They rode across town to
Snootington-on-the-Sea. Jasper did
most of the work since Scruff's paws
barely reached the pedals.

YE OLDE FUDGE SHOPPE

FUDGE
FLAVOR
OF THE DAY
COTTON CANDY.

Out of breath, Jasper stopped by a cheerily painted boat tied to the pier, beside a large wooden ice-cream cone.

"Ahoy, me hearties. What can I get ye on this fine day?" asked Salty Sid, leaning out of a porthole.

"We'll take all of your salted caramel
ice cream, please," said Scruff.

"ALL of it?" asked Salty Sid.

"Yes, ALL of it, please," said Jasper.
"And two spoons."

The pair ate

and ate

and ate.

Finally, they reached the bottom
of the tub. Jasper's head throbbed,
and his tummy ached.

"What if we *never* find the
Golden Bone?" he groaned.

But Scruff wasn't listening.
Buzzing from all the sugar, he zipped
around in circles chasing his ball.

The ball knocked into the wooden
cone. It wobbled and then...

Ker-*thunk!*

The wooden cone tipped over, and the scoop of ice cream bounced away.

Something was taped to the inside of the cone. Scruff picked it up with his teeth and dropped it into Jasper's lap.

"Eww!" said Jasper.
"It's covered in drool!"

"It's a key!" said Scruff. "Maybe it opens a treasure chest."

"And look, there's another clue," said Jasper. "Do you mind if we take this, Sid?"

"Not at all," replied Sid. "Ye have just bought a week's worth of ice cream. I'd be happy to help."

Jasper read the clue:

A place of curtains, lights, and magic,
For those who enjoy all things dramatic.
Tread the boards until they squeak—
You will find the treasure
that you seek.

"Lights, curtains, drama...," said
Jasper. "I know this one. It has to be
the Velvet Theater!" He even knew a
way to get in from his acting days.
"You were right, Scruff. This is fun!
Now, let's get back on that bike."

Before long, they arrived at the
theater. Jasper leaned the bike against
a lamppost and led the way around the
back. He pulled away some ivy
to reveal a door.

Jasper stepped inside and reached
for a switch on the wall. *Click!*

A bright spotlight illuminated the stage.
They stepped out from the wings.

"We need to find the squeak," said
Scruff, jumping on the wooden floor.
He stomped up and down until...

Eeeeeee! a floorboard squeaked.

"That's it!" cried Jasper, his tail
flicking back and forth with
excitement.

Scruff sniffed around. "There's a
handle here," he said. "Help me pull!"

45

They pulled and pulled,
and finally it gave way.

"A trapdoor!" they said together,
peering into the darkness below.

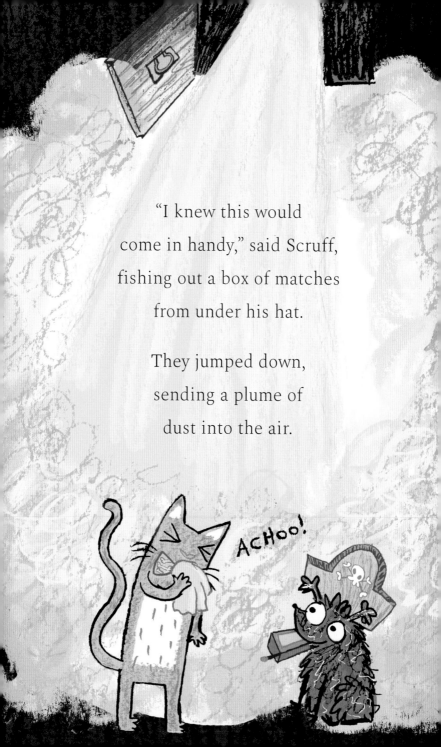

"I knew this would come in handy," said Scruff, fishing out a box of matches from under his hat.

They jumped down, sending a plume of dust into the air.

ACHOO!

As Jasper lit a match, Scruff ran on ahead.

The puppy stopped by a pile of masks
and bejeweled costumes. He then
started to try things on.

"Look at me!" he said, twirling in a circle.

"The treasure could be just around the corner, Scruff," said Jasper, rolling his eyes. "You can play dress-up later."

"Okay, fine," said Scruff, stuffing some costumes under his hat.

Jasper lit another match.
He spotted a large wooden treasure
chest with a gold trim.

"That has to be it!" he said, hurrying
over. Scruff skidded to a halt beside him
and passed him the key.

Jasper slid the key into the lock and
turned it carefully. Then he lifted the lid.

Creeeak!

Holding his breath, Scruff
peered inside. But it was empty
except for a slip of paper.

"Oh, not another clue,"
moaned Jasper. "We really do
need to get back to the store."

He lit another match
and read out loud:

Three hooded figures loomed through
the trapdoor above them.

"Who are you?" Jasper demanded.

"Grrrrrrr!" growled Scuff,
baring his teeth.

"Hello, darlings,"
trilled a familiar voice.

"Lady Catterly!" Jasper hissed as the
figure lowered her hood.

The other figures lowered
their hoods, too.

"Reginald and Oswald!" barked Scruff.

"And here we leave you two alone,
because there is no Golden Bone!"
squealed Lady Catterly.

The Sophisticats grinned down at them.
Then the trapdoor slammed shut.

"Nooooo!" howled Scruff.

"We're trapped," muttered Jasper. *The*
Sophisticats must've hatched this plan to
get revenge for my dinner party, he thought.
After all, they did end up eating cake
covered in puppy hair and drool.

The last match burned out, and the pair
was plunged into the inky darkness.

Jasper tried to think of
an escape plan. But the
trapdoor was too high up.

"I smell hot dogs," said
Scruff, interrupting
Jasper's thoughts.

"Hot dogs?" said Jasper.
"How can you think of
your stomach, Scruff?
We have to find a way out."

But Scruff scurried off.

"Here!" said the puppy. He nudged the back wall, and a panel fell open.

"Good job, Scruff!" Jasper cried.

They squeezed through the gap and found themselves in a metal pipe.

"I think we're in an air vent,"
said Jasper. "Just follow your nose."

They crawled along and then
climbed upward until....

"I *see* hot dogs!" barked Scruff
as he reached a grate.

He pushed it open and tumbled out into
the lobby, right in front of some hot dogs.

Jasper was close behind.

"Thank goodness!" he said, dusting himself
off and straightening his bow tie.

"Two hot dogs, please,"
said Scruff.

Scruff gulped down his hot dog
happily, while Jasper picked at his
with a knife and fork.

"Now, can we get back to our bookstore?" said Jasper, handing the rest of his hot dog to Scruff.

"Yum! More for me!" said Scruff as he followed Jasper outside.

THE VELVET THEATER

CAT ON A HOT TIN ROOF

The town clock chimed three
as they reached the Paw and Tail.

Jasper was just about to unlock
the door when a dark shadow
fell over him.

They looked up to see
two enormous gorillas.

"It seems you are trespassing,"
said one.

"Trespassing?" said Jasper,
raising an eyebrow. "This is our store,
I'll have you know."

GRRRRR

"I think you'll find it's under new
ownership," said the other gorilla,
pointing at the window.

Inside, Lady Catterly sat with her feet propped on the counter, a key dangling from a chain around her neck.

Oswald was chewing toffee and leafing through a book with his sticky paws.

Reginald poked at a display with his umbrella, knocking some books to the floor.

Jasper let out a groan. *So that's why they tricked us. They wanted our store!*

"We'd best be sending you on your way," the gorillas said together.

Jasper and Scruff were lifted high in the air and landed in a heap by the curb.

Head spinning, Jasper sat up
slowly to see a pair of boots with
shiny buckles in front of him.
A gloved paw helped him to his feet.

"It seems we have something
in common," said the cat in
a voice as velvet as her hat.
"Lady Catterly has stolen from us."

"Black Whiskers!"

exclaimed Scruff, getting to his feet.

"I thought you were lost at sea,"
said Jasper.

"I was. I sailed on three different
ships, on seven different seas, to make
it back here. Is there somewhere we
can talk?" the pirate asked.

Back at Jasper and Scruff's apartment,
over steaming mugs of catnip tea, Black
Whiskers explained how she and Lady
Catterly had once been friends.

"I loved discovering new lands," said
the pirate, "while Lady Catterly loved
shopping for precious spices,
silk, and jewelery.

"Then we heard about the
treasure on Dogtooth Island."
Her green eyes narrowed.

"It was protected by a giant octopus,"
Black Whiskers went on, adjusting
the sword on her belt. "I battled the
creature and won, of course."

"But while I was busy fighting,
Lady Catterly stole the Golden Bone
and sailed away with my ship!"

"So Lady Catterly has the Golden Bone?" gasped Scruff.

Black Whiskers nodded. "Yes, I've heard that she wears it to special events."

"Well, then," said Jasper, opening his notebook. "I have a plan."

Later that day, an invitation arrived at
The Sophisticats' headquarters.

Intimate concert with

Alvis Pawsley at

exclusive new venue:

The Gilded Kipper

Snootington-on-the-Sea pier

7 p.m.

Only the
most fabulous
allowed admission

RSVP

"I suppose we can make an appearance," Lady Catterly purred.

Reginald and Oswald nodded.

"The Sophisticats expect the full V.I.P. treatment, of course," she added.

That evening, disguised in the theater costumes, Jasper and Scruff watched through a porthole as The Sophisticats arrived. As Lady Catterly walked up the red carpet to *The Gilded Kipper*, something glittered between her ears.

"The Golden Bone!" Scruff nudged Jasper. "It's on Lady Catterly's tiara."

"A fishing boat, how quaint," said Lady Catterly, stepping aboard. "I've been on far more impressive vessels on my travels."

"Seen it before," said Reginald, yawning.

"I hope there's food,"
said Oswald, licking his lips.

As Salty Sid steered the boat out
to sea, Jasper served drinks while
Scruff handed out snacks.

"What are we waiting for?"
whined Lady Catterly.
"We want Alvis!"

"Alvis! Alvis!" shouted Reginald.

"The cocktail sausages are all gone!"
grumbled Oswald.

"If you'll kindly come this way,
I will now take you to see Alvis," Jasper
said. "You just need to walk across here."
He gestured to a narrow plank of wood.

"This is outrageous!"
yowled Lady Catterly.

"It's awfully dark," said Oswald.

"I'm not sure about this,"
muttered Reginald.

"All part of the surprise," said Jasper.
"We've just arrived at a private island
for the concert."

"Well, it does sound exclusive," said
Lady Catterly, brightening.

The Sophisticats reached the
end of the plank.

"I don't see an island...," said Lady
Catterly uneasily. "Just water."

"Yes," said Black Whiskers, leaping
out of the shadows. "There is an island
nearby, but you'll have to swim for it."

"YOU!" shrieked Lady Catterly. "What are YOU doing here?"

"Nice to see you, too, old friend. Before you go, I'll take this."

The pirate lifted the key from Lady Catterly's neck with a flick of her sword.

Swish!

"And my treasure," Black Whiskers
added, snatching the tiara from
Lady Catterly's head.

Startled, Lady Catterly fell backward,
pulling Reginald and Oswald with her.

Splash!

The three cats flailed around in the water.

Jasper and Scruff removed their
disguises and waved down at them.
"See you later!" they called.

"We'll get you for this!"
screeched Lady Catterly.

As the friends sailed back to shore,
they could hear the howls of
The Sophisticats on the wind.

The next day, Jasper and Scruff held a grand
reopening party at the Paw and Tail.

As guest of honor, Black Whiskers
thrilled everyone with tales of her
adventures at sea.

Alvis Pawsley sang some of
his greatest hits.

Salty Sid served his
famous ice cream.

It was a wonderful evening.
The entire town was invited,
except for three snooty cats.

Jasper went to find Scruff. "Time to crack open the sparkling catnip juice, I think. That was a lot of fun, even though it didn't go quite as planned. I hope we can go on more adventures together."

"Yes! Me, too!" said Scruff, wagging his tail.